W9-CTU-287

Editor: Leone Peguero
Cover Illustration: Terry Riley
Illustrations: Jan Scherpenhuizen
Typesetting: Midland Typesetters

Treasure Island
First published in 2008 by
Playmore Inc., Publishers,
58 Main Street, Hackensack, N.J. 07601

Printed in China

TREASURE ISLAND

ROBERT LOUIS STEVENSON

The Author
Robert Louis Stevenson
(1850–1894)

Robert Louis Stevenson wrote *Treasure Island* for his young stepson. It was published in 1883 and has been famous ever since.

Stevenson was born in Edinburgh, Scotland, in 1850. He was the son of an engineer and studied law before deciding to become a writer.

Treasure Island was his first full-length novel. It was followed by several other popular stories, including *The Strange Case of Dr. Jekyll and Mr. Hyde*, *Kidnapped*, and *The Master of Ballantrae*.

All of his most famous books have been adapted for television or the movies.

Stevenson, who was also a travel writer and poet, died aged 44.

Contents

Glossary

Pirates and sailors had a language of their own.
You will find these words in the story:

buccaneer	a name for a pirate
cat-o'-nine tails	a whip with nine straps
crow's nest	a place on top of a mast where sailors kept a lookout
cutlass	the pirate's favorite sword
Davy Jones's Locker	the bottom of the sea, where sailors go when they die
galley	a ship's kitchen
gentleman of fortune	another name for a pirate
hammock	a hanging bed where sailors sleep on ships
keelhaul	to tie a man up and haul him under the boat as a punishment

Treasure Island

landlubber	someone who has never been to sea
maroon	to leave someone alone on a deserted island
pieces of eight	old Spanish coins
pigtail	hair tied back in a bunch
rigging	ropes attached to a ship's masts and sails
sea chest	a trunk used by sailors to store their belongings
sea dog	an old sailor or pirate
shanty	sea song
tattoo	a picture painted with ink on someone's skin
walk the plank	force an enemy to walk along a beam of wood until they fall into the sea

Introduction
Billy Bones, Flint, and Jim Hawkins

Captain Billy Bones is my name. No pirate ever killed or robbed as many people as me . . . except old Captain Flint, of course.

Flint was a cruel buccaneer. Hundreds he killed. He hanged 'em, made 'em walk the plank, keelhauled 'em till they drowned, or stuck 'em with his cutlass.

I was one of Flint's pirates. I was on his ship, *The Walrus,* on the day he went ashore on a deserted island to bury his fabulous treasure.

Old Flint took six sailors with him to help him bury it, but he came back all alone. He must have murdered them and buried them with his treasure.

He never told any of us where he hid that treasure; nor how he killed those sailors.

Much later he fell sick. He'd drunk too much rum. I was with him the day he went to Davy Jones's Locker. That, for you yellow-livered landlubbers, is the bottom of the sea where sailors go when they die.

I'll never forget his last words. "Get me a rum, Billy Bones," he said. "Just one last rum, for an old sea dog."

I went below decks to get him his rum.

By the time I returned, old Flint was dead and lying on his back with a map clenched in his fist.

The whole crew had gathered around him. You never did see a more terrifying gang of pirates.

None of 'em had everything they were born with. Some had eyes missing, others had lost a leg or an arm, or just a few fingers. Most of 'em were scarred where other pirates had taken bits out of them with a cutlass. Others had terrible scars where Flint's cat-o'-nine-tails had whipped them.

They weren't fools though. They all tried to grab the map in Flint's hand.

I slashed at them with my cutlass and cut off two of Black Dog's fingers. That stopped them in their tracks. I was the captain now that Flint was gone. The map was mine by right.

"Don't worry, me lads," I said, "I'll treat you fair. If this 'ere map shows where Flint's

The crew gathered around him.

3

treasure is, I'll share it with every one of you. That's my promise."

But what's the good of a pirate's promise, eh? That night I filled my sea chest with all my possessions, a bag of Flint's gold coins, and the map. And while my shipmates snored away, I jumped ship.

I lowered my sea chest into one of the ship's small boats and rowed ashore.

I landed in a cove on the south coast of England and went to look for a place where I could hide from my old shipmates for a while.

I found a lonely place called the Admiral Benbow Inn. It was run by a woman and her fourteen-year-old son, a fine young lad called Jim Hawkins.

My plan was to lie low for a while and then get another crew to set sail in search of Flint's treasure. For sure, the map would lead me straight to it.

But, like Old Flint, my fondness for the rum got the better of me. I'll not live long enough to find the treasure now . . .

But perhaps young Jim Hawkins will find my map. Then he can tell the rest of this story about the hunt for Flint's treasure.

And he'll tell it true . . . which is more than a lying, murdering pirate like me could ever do.

Chapter 1
Jim Hawkins Begins his Story

I'll never forget the night I first met that blood-thirsty pirate, Billy Bones. I didn't know his name then. He didn't want anyone to know who he was.

A great storm was blowing in from the sea. The wind was shaking all four walls of the Admiral Benbow Inn where I lived with my mother.

I was watching the huge waves rolling into the bay from my bedroom window.

Suddenly, a flash of lightning lit the road below the inn. I saw a figure and then it was gone again, swallowed in the blackness. I thought I'd seen a ghost.

Then, between the rolls of thunder, I heard a man singing an old pirate shanty.

"Fifteen men on a dead man's chest,
Yo-ho-ho and a bottle of rum!"

A man was coming up the hill. At last, I saw him come stumbling out of the blackness. He had a big stick in one hand and was dragging an old sea chest behind him with the other.

Moments later the inn door shook as if it had been hit with two thunderbolts. The visitor had given the door two bangs with his stick. "Open up, you landlubbers," his voice roared, "a man needs a splash or two of rum on a night like this."

I opened the door. Our visitor was a tall man with a dark, weather-beaten face and a vivid red scar across his right cheek.

His dark, oily hair was tied in a pigtail, which fell across his shoulder. He was wearing a filthy blue coat and carried a cutlass, knife, and pistol in his belt. He was clearly a seaman of some sort.

"A drink, lad, and quick. A man could die in this weather," he snorted, dropping his sea chest in a corner of the room and then asking me my name.

"Jim Hawkins," I replied.

"Well, Master Hawkins, do you have many visitors here?" he asked as I poured him the rum.

"No," I said. "This is a lonely inn. A few people pass by on their way to Bristol."

"That's all good and shipshape for me,

A man came up the hill.

matey," growled the man. "I'm not wanting to see any strangers . . . or old friends for that matter."

I asked him how long he wanted to stay.

"That's for me to know, not you," said the man, pulling a small pouch from his pocket.

He carefully picked out four gold pieces and threw them on the table. "That'll do for now. Just tell me when I've spent that lot."

That night he sat down in a corner of the parlor, facing the door. On the table in front of him were his four constant friends . . . a glass of rum, his pistol, knife, and cutlass.

"If you want a name for me, just call me Captain," he said to me.

The captain's eyes were fixed on the door. He was clearly expecting trouble to come through it.

Chapter 2
A Lookout for the One-legged Man

During the daytime, the captain spent most of his time lurking around the cove or walking on the cliffs. His cutlass would be swinging beneath his old blue seaman's coat, his hat tilted on his head, and a brass telescope under his arm.

Every so often he would look through his telescope and search the horizon.

When he returned to the inn, he would always ask me the same question. "Have you seen any sailors about today, Jim?"

I thought he was missing his old shipmates and hoping some would pass this way.

One day a seaman did come to stay. The captain became very suspicious. He would not come into the room until he had peeped through the door first.

He didn't like anyone asking him questions, either. If someone did, he got very angry and blew through his nose like a foghorn.

That was enough to scare anyone away.

He seemed to trust me though. Maybe it was because I was young.

"Jim Hawkins, young mate," he said, "I want you to keep a careful watch for a seafaring man. If he comes, he'll come a-hopping. He's only got one leg. I'll pay you to look out for him."

He then grabbed my arm and pulled me close. "But don't tell a soul about what I've asked you to do, or else you'll get this," he hissed, pointing to his knife. "Just let me know as soon as you see that one-legged devil."

The thought of the one-legged sailor haunted me. In the dead of night, I could see him a thousand times in my dreams. Sometimes his leg would be cut off at the knee, then at the hip. Then he might be a monster with one leg in the middle of his body. In my worst nightmares, he would come leaping after me on the cliffs.

Most nights the captain drank too much and the inn shook as he sang wild sea songs. Then he'd call for everyone to have a drink with him. And most nights he told savage stories about hangings, sailors walking the plank, and terrible storms at sea.

Jim's worst nightmares.

My mother and I were afraid that the captain would ruin our inn. People were staying away for fear of the man and his stories.

Week after week, he stayed with us. The four gold coins he had given were soon used up. But he never paid us another. When my mother asked for money, the captain just blew down his nose with a great roar. She never dared ask him again after that.

He never changed the clothes he wore. Some were almost in rags. His hat finally blew apart one stormy day. But he still wore it like a shipwreck on his head. He patched up his old coat so many times that, in the end, it was nothing but patches.

As for the sea chest he had brought with him, no one had ever seen that opened. It never left his room. I often wondered what was hidden inside.

Chapter 3
Visitors at the Admiral Benbow

The captain used the Admiral Benbow Inn as if it was his ship. We were his crew. We all did as he told us, everyone that is, except Doctor Livesey.

One day, the good doctor came to visit the inn when the drunken captain was singing his song about fifteen men on a dead man's chest.

The doctor started talking to my mother. The captain didn't like it when people talked while he was singing.

"Silence below decks, landlubber!" he shouted at the doctor.

"Were you talking to me, sir?" said Doctor Livesey, calmly.

"I was," roared the captain.

"You drunken fool," said the doctor. "Carry on drinking so much rum and the world will soon be rid of you."

The captain's face flushed red with anger.

He sprang to his feet, dagger in hand, threatening to pin the doctor to the wall.

Doctor Livesey did not move. He spoke to the captain quietly and firmly. "If you don't put that knife away this instant, I shall see you hanged. I am not only a doctor but also a magistrate. What do you say to that?"

The captain put away his weapon and sat down, grumbling like a dog.

"Sir, I shall be keeping an eye on you," said the doctor. "If I hear of any trouble, I'll have you hunted down."

The captain didn't speak for days after that.

***

Soon after, another stranger arrived at the Admiral Benbow Inn. The new visitor was a pale, tall character, also wearing a cutlass on his belt. He was missing two fingers on his left hand. Thankfully, he had both of his legs.

I had just laid the table for the captain's breakfast and the man pointed to it. "Is this here table for my mate, Bill?"

I told the man that I didn't know anyone called Bill, but there was a man we called the captain.

Threatening the doctor

"That would be my mate Captain Billy Bones," he sneered. "Where is the old devil?"

I said that the captain was on the beach and would be back soon.

That seemed to please him. He stood behind the inn door, occasionally peering around it to see if anyone was coming. He was like a cat waiting for a mouse.

Once I stepped outside to see if the captain was on his way. The man quickly hauled me back and shook me. "Stay inside, young 'un," he threatened, "or something might happen to you."

We heard the sound of the captain's footsteps approaching the inn. The man glanced out of the door and then quickly hid himself behind it.

"Yes, that be my old mate, Captain Billy Bones," said the man. "Bless his old heart to be sure. Now you and me, lad, we'll just give Bill a little surprise."

Then he pushed his coat aside and took hold of his gleaming cutlass.

"We'll just give Bill a little surprise."

Chapter 4
Black Dog

The captain strode into the inn, slammed the door behind him, and marched straight to his breakfast table. He sat down, with his back to where we were hiding.

"Hello, Bill," said the stranger.

The captain spun round. His face had gone pale, as if he had heard a ghost.

"Come on, Billy Bones, surely you remember an old shipmate."

The captain gasped. "Black Dog!"

"And who else?" roared the man. "Black Dog, indeed. Old Black Dog's come to find his shipmate, Billy."

He held up his left hand. "It's not been so long since you cut off these two fingers, eh? And then you jumped ship. That wasn't a very friendly thing to do, was it?"

The captain glared at the man. "So you've found me, Black Dog. Speak up! What do you want?"

Chased by the captain.

19

"First, let's share a glass or two of rum," he said, looking at me. "This dear boy will get that for us. Then we'll talk square, like old shipmates."

When I returned with the rum, they were seated at the breakfast table. Black Dog was next to the door. It looked as if he was keeping one eye on the captain and another on an escape route.

"Leave us now, sonny," he said, "and don't go listening through the keyhole."

I hurried away. But I did try and listen to what they were saying. At first, they were whispering. Gradually, the voices got louder. They started to argue and curse.

The captain shouted, "If I hang, then I'll take you all with me."

I heard the table and chairs go over, a clash of steel, and a cry of pain.

I looked through the keyhole and saw Black Dog being chased by the captain. He had his cutlass raised and Black Dog's shoulder was streaming blood.

Black Dog was out of the door when the captain slashed at him again. The blow would have cut him in two. Instead, the cutlass sliced into the signpost of the Admiral Benbow Inn.

A heavy fall.

To this very day, you can see the mark that blade carved.

The blow was the last of the battle. Black Dog scuttled away and disappeared over the hill.

The captain leaned against the wall by the door, panting hard. "Rum," he cried, "then I must get away from here."

As I went to get the rum, I heard a heavy fall. I ran back and found the captain lying stretched out on the floor. He was breathing loud and hard. His eyes were closed. His face was a horrible blue.

My mother rushed in. "Is he dead?" she cried.

Luckily, Doctor Livesey appeared through the door at that moment.

"The man's been injured," said my mother.

"Fiddle-faddle," said the doctor. "He's dying of the rum. It has got to his heart. I warned him."

We took the captain to his room and laid him on the bed. Soon after, he recovered a little and called out, "Black Dog! Where's Black Dog?"

Doctor Livesey told him that he'd gone. The captain relaxed a little.

"Rum will be the death of you," said the doctor.

The captain didn't reply. He had turned over and fallen asleep.

That's when I saw he had a seaman's tattoo painted on his shoulder. It was a picture of a gallows. A man was hanging from it.

Chapter 5
Captain Flint's Secret

The next morning I visited the captain in his room. He was awake.

"Bring me a rum, Jim," he begged.

"The doctor said you mustn't have any."

"What do I care!" he said. "What does that landlubber know? I've been in places as hot as hell. I've seen earthquakes. I've lived on rum. It's meat and drink to me. If I don't have me rum, it'll be the death of me."

His hands were shaking. "I've got the horrors of Old Captain Flint running around in my head," he moaned. "He was in my dreams last night."

I had never heard of Flint before. But, whoever he was, his name brought a look of terror to the captain's eyes.

I wasn't brave enough to refuse the captain his rum. He swallowed it greedily.

"Black Dog, he's a bad 'un," the captain said. "If I don't get away, he and his gang are sure to kill me."

"Why?" I asked.

"It's my sea chest they are after," he said. "There are dark secrets in there. Flint was an old pirate and I was one of his crew, along with Black Dog and that man with the one leg."

I shivered at the thought of the one-legged man and wondered if he would be the next man to visit our inn.

"Old Flint gave me his secret when he died," continued the captain. "There's others who will say I stole it. What's the difference? Flint's secret is well hidden in my sea chest. That's what they're after. And they'll kill me to get it."

The captain's voice grew weaker. "Jim, you must watch out for Black Dog. He may come again. And keep a lookout for that one-legged man too."

Then the captain fell asleep.

I told no one what he had said. I was too scared that he might wake up and regret having told me so much. Then he might have cut me to pieces with his cutlass.

***

Next morning was bitter and frosty and I saw an old hunched figure slowly tap-tap-

tapping his way up the hill with a stick in front of him. He was plainly blind. He wore a tattered sea-cloak with a hood and, beneath it, his blinded eyes were hidden beneath a green shade.

He stopped by the door. "Will any kind friend help a poor blind man?" he cried. "Will anyone help a man who lost his eyes fighting for England and good King George?"

"Can I help?" I asked.

The man turned toward me. "Good young man, take my hand and lead me into the inn. This is the Admiral Benbow Inn, isn't it?"

He spoke in a gentle way. I felt sorry for him. "Yes it is," I answered.

I held out my hand to guide him inside.

The man gripped it like a vice. Now I saw his cruel, unseeing eyes beneath the hood. His face was twisted with hate.

I tried to escape, but he held on with an iron fist.

"Now," sneered the blind man, "take me to the captain. And when he sees me, say: 'Here's a friend to see you, Bill.' Do that, boy, or you're as dead as Flint."

I had never heard a voice so cold or ugly.

He was plainly blind.

Chapter 6
Blind Pew

I led the blind man into the parlor. The captain was sitting in his usual chair.

"Captain," I quaked, "there's a friend to see you."

The captain looked up. You would have thought he'd seen another ghost because his face turned as pale as when he had seen Black Dog.

"Now, Bill," said the blind man. "I may not be able to see you, but I can hear even a finger stirring. So stay where you are, unless you want to feel the blade of my cutlass."

The captain froze.

"Bill Bones," said the blind man. "You've got until ten o'clock tonight to give us the map you took from Captain Flint. You know what will happen to you if you don't."

The captain shivered.

"The men have passed a death sentence on you," said the blind man. "It's that or give us the map."

The captain put a hand to his throat.

Then he slid out of the room. I heard him tap-tap-tapping down the hill. I was never so happy in my life to see someone leave. He had made my legs tremble so much I could hardly stand.

The captain gathered his senses. "That was Blind Pew, another of Flint's old shipmates, damn him," he said. "Ten o'clock? That's six hours. I can be well gone by then."

The captain sprang to his feet. But he didn't get very far. He stood swaying for a moment and then put his hand to his throat. There was a gurgling sound. And then he fell backwards to the floor.

Blind Pew had frightened the captain to death.

***

After the captain's death, I told my mother everything that he had told me. She was worried for our safety, especially as Blind Pew and his crew would be back at ten o'clock.

We decided to get help from the village that lay in the cove beneath the inn. We ran all the way. Some people there told us that they had seen a strange ship drop anchor a few days

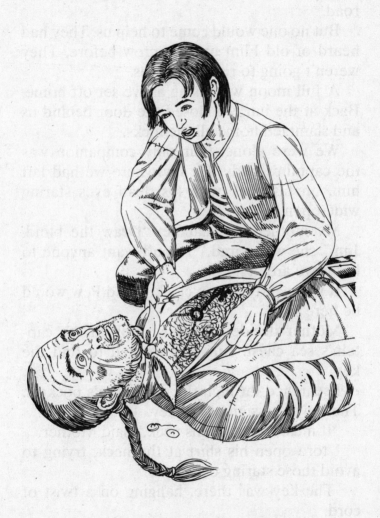

The key was round his neck.

earlier. They had also seen strangers on the road.

But no one would come to help us. They had heard of old Flint and his crew before. They weren't going to risk their lives.

A full moon was rising as we set off home. Back at the inn, we closed the door behind us and slammed home all the locks.

We were alone. Our only companion was the captain's body. He lay where we had left him, on his back with his dead eyes staring wide-open.

My mother lit a candle. "Draw the blind, Jim," she whispered, "I don't want anyone to know we are in here."

It was nearly nine o'clock. Blind Pew would be here soon.

Mother decided we must look in the captain's sea chest. But first we had to find the key.

I searched through the dead man's pockets. There was no sign of the key.

"It must be round his neck," said Mother.

I tore open his shirt at the neck, trying to avoid those staring dead eyes.

The key was there, hanging on a twist of cord.

Blind Pew

We hurried upstairs to the captain's old
room. The sea chest stood by the bed. The
initial "B" for Bones had been burned on
the top with a hot iron. The corners were all
smashed and broken from many a rough sea
voyage.

I put the key in the stiff lock, turned it, and
threw back the lid.

Chapter 7
The Captain's Sea Chest

A strong smell of tobacco rose from the sea chest as we opened it.

On top was a new suit of clothes, carefully brushed and folded. Beneath the suit were two fine pistols, a bar of silver, a Spanish clock, a pair of brass compasses, and some shiny sea-shells.

Farther down there was a faded cloak, salty white from the spray of the sea. Beneath that was a canvas bag. It jingled with the sound of coins. I emptied it onto the floor. Never had I seen so many gold coins!

Right at the bottom of the chest lay one last object. It was a small parcel wrapped in oilskin to keep it dry.

I was about to open it when I heard a sound. My heart leapt into my mouth.

I heard the tap-tap-tapping of Blind Pew's stick coming back up the hill again.

"Mother," I whispered, "let's be going."

Never had I seen so many gold coins!

Her face turned ashen. "Don't make a sound, Jim."

We held our breaths. We both jumped when a stick rapped against the front door.

There was a shout. "Open up!"

The handle turned and the bolt rattled.

There was a long silence. Finally, we heard the tap-tapping again. To our joy, Blind Pew was going away.

"We must get out of here," I cried. "He'll be back soon enough."

I picked up the oilskin packet. The next moment we were down the stairs and out of the door.

We darted across to some bushes opposite the inn and hid. My heart was thumping and my mother was out of breath with terror.

Then we saw three men running up the hill toward the inn. They were running together with their arms linked. As they moved closer, I saw that two of the men were carrying another between them. It was Blind Pew coming back again.

Blind Pew returns.

Chapter 8
The Last of Blind Pew

"Down with the door!" shrieked Pew.

Our hideaway was so close to the Admiral Benbow Inn that we could hear every word.

Two men rushed at the door with a huge log of wood and knocked it down. They disappeared inside, only to reappear moments later.

"Bill's dead," called one of them. "His body's here."

"Forget Bill," screamed Pew. "Bring the chest."

Soon after, the window to Captain Billy Bones's room was thrown open with a slam and a crashing of glass. One of the men leaned out into the moonlight.

"Someone's been here before us," he cried, "and searched the chest."

"Is the map there?" shouted Pew.

"No," replied the man.

Pew was almost foaming at the mouth with anger. "Search Bill's body."

Knocking the door down.

39

A moment later, the man reappeared at the window. "Someone's searched him too. There's nothing on him."

Pew was hysterical. "It's those people from the inn," he cried. "The boy Hawkins and his mother. They have it. I wish I had torn their eyes out. Scatter boys. Find 'em. Kill 'em if you have to."

I felt my mother shiver. Then we heard the piercing sound of a whistle.

Blind Pew must have left a man at the bottom of the hill to warn them if anyone was coming.

The men rushed out of the inn and raced away, leaving Pew behind.

"You cowards and villains," screamed Pew. "You ain't got the courage of a weevil in a stale biscuit."

Next I heard the sound of horses galloping up the hill. Pew panicked, blindly stumbling into bushes and ditches as he tried to get away. "You can't leave old Pew," he shouted at his cowardly mates, "not old Pew!"

Those were his last words. He ran straight into the path of the horses. Down he went with a terrible cry beneath the galloping hooves. Pew was dead, stone dead.

He ran straight into the horses.

The riders were Mr. Dance, the King's agent, and his men. They had heard about the ship anchored in the bay and thought the men were smugglers.

I told him that the others had run away.

"Then we'll go after them," he roared, turning his horse around.

Before he rode away, Mr. Dance asked me why the pirates had come to the inn.

"I think I have the answer in my pocket," I cried, "but I need to see Doctor Livesey first and tell him what I've found."

***

I rode hard to Doctor Livesey's house. He was talking with Squire John Trelawney when I arrived.

I told them I knew why Captain Bones's shipmates had dropped anchor in the bay and taken such an interest in Bill and our inn.

I pulled out the oilskin packet and handed it to Doctor Livesey.

The bundle was sewn together, so the doctor cut it with his medical scissors. There were two things inside, a book with the name Bill Bones written on the cover and a sealed paper.

It was a map.

The pages of the book were full of strange notes and names with crosses beside them. "This is the black-hearted scoundrel's account book," said the squire. "Here are the names of the ships Flint and Billy Bones and their men attacked."

"And now," said the doctor, "for the other object."

He opened the sealed paper with great care. It was a map. At the top were written two words: "Treasure Island".

Chapter 9
The Map of Treasure Island

The map showed Treasure Island was about nine miles long and five miles wide. At the top lay North Cove. In the middle was Spy Glass Hill and close by was a small cabin, surrounded by a wooden stockade.

There was a smaller piece of land just offshore from the main island. It was called Skeleton Island.

In the middle of the larger island a single red cross had been painted in blood, and beneath it, the words "Flint's treasure".

On the bottom of the map were some mysterious notes:

Start Skeleton Island. Big tree. North-west to Spy Glass Hill. Tall tree. Ten paces south.

And beneath those words was a signature: *James Flint.*

We all stood in stunned silence for a moment. We had Flint's treasure map and all the clues to find where it lay buried.

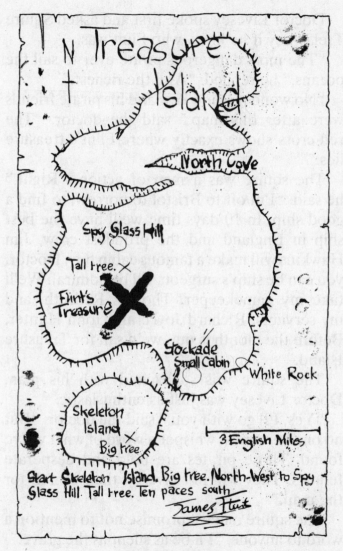

Treasure Island.

Doctor Livesey spoke first and asked Squire Trelawney if he knew who Flint was.

"The most dangerous pirate ever to sail the oceans," he replied. "And the richest."

"No wonder Blind Pew and his pirate friends were after this map," said the doctor. "The red cross shows exactly where Flint's treasure lies."

The squire was a man of action. "Right," he said, "I'm off to Bristol tomorrow, to find a good ship. In 10 days time we'll have the best ship in England and the proudest crew. Jim Hawkins will make a famous cabin boy. Doctor, you can be ship's surgeon. I'll be admiral. We'll take my gamekeeper, Thomas Redruth, and my servants, Richard Joyce and John Hunter. Before the month is out, we'll sail for Treasure Island."

The squire was so excited with his plan. Doctor Livesey was just as enthusiastic.

"Yes, I'll go with you," said the doctor. "But no one here must whisper a word of what we've found. Those pirates are bold and desperate fellows. They will not give up their search for the map."

The squire made a promise not to mention a word to anyone. "I'll be as silent as the grave."

***

Three weeks later a letter arrived at the Admiral Benbow Inn. It was from the squire.

His news was that he had found a ship, the *Hispaniola*. It had been fitted out and was ready for sea.

The squire also said he had found a crew. He mentioned one man in particular who was going to be the ship's cook.

He runs an inn, he wrote, *but he is a true seafaring fellow. Poor fellow only has one leg and lost it fighting for his king and country. I hired him at once. Long John Silver is his name.*

He has also found me some of the toughest old salts for a crew. They might not be pretty to look at, but their faces are enough to scare off even the ghost of Captain Flint.

I stopped reading the letter. A one-legged man? I was afraid that Long John Silver was the same man Captain Billy Bones had asked me to watch out for. But when I thought of the adventure before me, I forgot my fears.

The next day I set off with Redruth in a coach bound for Bristol. My mother was sad to see me go. But she knew Doctor Livesey would look after me.

As the Admiral Benbow Inn disappeared from sight, I wondered if I would ever see my mother or my old home again.

One of my last thoughts was of Captain Billy Bones. I thought of him striding along the beach with his cocked hat, his scar, and his old brass telescope.

We reached Bristol that evening and were met by Squire Trelawney.

The place was full of sailors. Most of them wore rings in their ears, whiskers curled to their chin, and long pigtails.

The squire said I should go to bed early that night because we were to sail the next day.

But as it was still light, he said I could go and meet the ship's cook, Long John Silver.

"You'll like him," said the squire. "A real old salt. You'll find him at the Spy Glass Inn."

Chapter 10
Long John Silver

Long John Silver's place was the busiest inn I had ever seen. I thought it strange, though, that it was called the Spy Glass, the same name as the highest hill on the Treasure Island map.

The place was full of sailors sitting around bare, wooden, candlelit tables. Most were smoking pipes and drinking. I could hardly see across the room for smoke. Some of the sailors were singing sea shanties.

No sooner had I entered the inn than a man came toward me. He was hopping more than walking.

This was Long John Silver. His left leg had been cut off close by the hip and he carried a crutch under his shoulder. He hopped about like a bird on that crutch.

I was still wondering if Mr. Silver might turn out to be Captain Billy Bones's one-legged sailor. But one look was enough to make me change my mind.

I had seen Black Dog and Blind Pew, so I knew what a pirate looked like. This man was very different. He was cleanly dressed and was smiling. He was tall and very strong, with a face as big as a ham. He was intelligent and always happy. He whistled wherever he went.

The only unusual thing about him was that he had a screeching green parrot that perched on his shoulder.

"So pleased to see you, Jim Hawkins," said Silver, warmly shaking my hand.

Just then, a man rushed for the door.

"Stop him!" I shouted. "It's Black Dog."

"Black who?" asked Silver.

"Black Dog," I repeated. "One of the pirates who came to our inn."

Silver immediately ordered two friends to chase after Black Dog. He seemed very upset. "I will not have pirates in here," he said. "There was a blind man here once. When I found out he was a pirate, I sent him packing. They tell me he was run down by a horse."

"That was Blind Pew," I said. "I met him too."

"That was his name, my clever lad," cried Silver, patting me on the back. "I reckon you'd spot a pirate a mile off, eh?"

The place was full of sailors.

Jim meets Long John Silver.

The men came back soon after, both out of breath. They had lost the trail of Black Dog in a crowd.

I was beginning to think Long John Silver would make a good shipmate. He seemed to like me too.

"You're as smart as paint, Jim Hawkins," he laughed. "I saw that when you first came in. You and me shall get along fine. As smart as paint, that's what you are."

Chapter 11
Preparing to Sail

Squire Trelawney had named himself as the admiral of our ship, the *Hispaniola*. But the man really in charge was Captain Alexander Smollett.

"I don't like the sound of this voyage," Smollett said to the squire as soon as we came aboard the next morning. "You never told me we were going on a treasure hunt. Yet every other man knows it. I've heard the crew talking."

"Silver's parrot must have been squawking," said the squire.

We all knew who the loose talker was. People had told me that the squire could never keep a secret.

"I've heard," Captain Smollett added, "that you have a map of an island and that there is a cross which marks where the treasure is buried."

"I never told that to a soul," protested the squire.

"I don't like the sound of this voyage."

"The crew knows it," said the captain, "and the men could well mutiny and kill for a treasure map."

There was much work to do that morning. The last supplies were brought aboard and stored below deck.

Long John Silver was the last of the crew to arrive. He hopped aboard with his parrot on his shoulder.

Captain Smollett ordered him down to the cook's galley. "Take young Jim Hawkins with you to help," he said.

As we walked along the deck, Long John started singing a song I knew well.

"Fifteen men on a dead man's chest . . ."

From high on the rigging came a chorus from the crew preparing the sails for the journey.

"Yo-ho-ho and a bottle of rum."

Chapter 12

The Voyage to Treasure Island

So the *Hispaniola* set sail for Treasure Island.

Long John Silver proved to be a remarkable man. Having one leg was no problem for him. He carried his crutch on a rope around his neck. That way he had both hands free to do his cooking. Even with his crutch, he could move as fast as any other man on board.

"He's no ordinary man," said Israel Hands, who was Silver's closest shipmate. "He's smart and braver than a lion."

All the crew looked up to Silver. He was only the ship's cook but all the men saw him as their leader.

Silver had his way of saying things to people that made them feel good. He would tell them they were the best of shipmates, none better on the high seas.

He was always very kind to me and never stopped telling me that I was as "smart as paint".

"Young Jim Hawkins," he would say, "come

The Hispaniola.

and have a yarn with Long John. There's nobody I'd rather talk to than you, Jim. My parrot would like a yarn with you too."

Silver called his parrot Cap'n Flint after the infamous pirate. He told me that the parrot was two hundred years old. I was never quite sure whether to believe him.

Quite often, he'd talk with his parrot and ask it how the voyage was going.

The parrot would screech back at him. "Gold and silver. Pieces of eight! Gold and silver. Pieces of eight!"

Then Silver would ruffle his parrot's feathers.

It made me think he was the best of men.

The voyage went well. Within a few weeks, Captain Smollett told us we would soon sight the island.

***

One evening after sundown, I went looking for an apple to eat. All the fruit was kept in great wooden barrels on the main deck.

When I got there I could see that there were only one or two apples left and they were right at the bottom.

I leaned in headfirst to try and reach them. The sea wasn't rough that night, but the gentle rolling of the waves was enough to make me lose my balance; I tumbled to the bottom of the barrel.

Before I could recover my senses, I heard two men walking down the deck. They stopped by the barrel and started talking.

One of the men was Silver. The other was a young sailor called Dick. From my hiding place, I listened to what they were saying.

Silver was actually leaning against the barrel as he started to speak. He was so close I could smell the tobacco smoke from his pipe.

"I'll tell you a little about myself, Dick," he said, his voice changing to a whisper. "I served with Captain Flint on his ship *The Walrus*. Old Pew and Black Dog were with us too. Pew wasn't blind then. He still had his eyes and I had both my legs. Do you know, boy, a ship fired on us one day and took my leg away and Pew's eyes with the same cannon ball."

"That was unfortunate," said Dick.

"Hardly," said Silver. "The decks of the old *Walrus* were always awash with blood and stolen gold in those days. We killed many a man and we took plenty of gold. That's how I could afford to buy my inn."

I was shocked to hear what he was saying; I couldn't believe it at first.

"Us pirates, or gentlemen of fortune as I like to call 'em," went on Silver, "we live rough and risk a good hanging. But we fill our sea chests with gold. After this voyage I'll have enough gold to live like a true gentleman for the rest of my days. You can do the same, you know."

Now I truly saw that the man who had been so kind to me was a monstrous and bloody pirate, and a mighty cunning one at that.

I could see that Silver was trying to tempt Dick into becoming a pirate. He almost made

Hiding in the barrel

it sound an honest life.

But what he told Dick next really made me angry. "Dick, my boy," he said, "you and me should get on well. As smart as paint, that's what you are."

He had often said exactly the same words to me.

I was shaking with fear in the barrel now. Any moment Silver might look down and see me.

"Right you are," Silver said. "You're a brave lad, Dick, and smart too. Now, be off and think about what I've said. It would be best to join us, I promise you."

As soon as Dick was gone, Silver gave a low whistle and another man came to join him by the barrel.

I heard the man spit on the deck and then ask Silver a question. "When are we going to kill Captain Smollett and his mob? Tonight?"

It was Israel Hands. My blood ran cold. They were going to murder us all.

"Be patient," snarled Silver. "You never did have much of a brain, did yer? Big ears, yes, but no brain. Now listen with those great ears of yours. We need that map first."

"Then what?" asked Hands.

"Some might say it's best to put the squire and his shipmates ashore on a desert island," said Silver, "and leave 'em stranded until they die of starvation."

"No! No!" cried Hands. "I'd cut 'em up like roast pork with a cutlass. Billy Bones was the man for that. He always said that dead men can't bite. Let me kill Smollett. He's the one for me."

"Then I'll wring the head off the squire," sneered Silver, "or keelhaul him until he drowns."

As the two pirates walked away, I could hear them laughing.

Just then the moon came out from behind a cloud and lit up the top of the main mast.

From the bottom of the barrel, I looked up to the top of the mast where a sailor was on lookout duty in the crow's nest.

I saw him raise his arm and point into the distance.

"Land ho!" he cried. "It's Treasure Island! Land ho!"

Chapter 13
Treasure Island

The cry of "Land ho!" brought everyone rushing up onto the deck for their first sight of Treasure Island.

I climbed out of the barrel to see for myself. But what I had just overheard from Silver and Hands took away all the excitement I might have felt at seeing the island. All I wanted to do was to tell someone my news. The lives of honest men now depended on me.

But there was no time at present. The *Hispaniola* was about to drop anchor.

The ship came to rest in a channel midway between Treasure Island and Skeleton Island. She anchored just a few hundred yards off the sandy beach of the main island.

Behind the beach was a thick swamp. The place would be swarming with deadly snakes, warned the doctor.

Behind the swamp, thick belts of trees ran all the way up to the bare rocky summit of Spy

"It's Treasure Island!"

Glass Hill. It must have been some 400 feet tall. It was the highest place on the island.

As soon as the sails were down, I went looking for Doctor Livesey. I found him talking with Captain Smollett, the squire, and Long John Silver.

I shuddered when Silver put his hand around my shoulder. How many men had that hand killed?

"Ah, Jim my lad, just look," said Silver, pointing to the island. "What a wonderful place. You can swim and climb them hills like a mountain goat. I remember when I was young and had ten toes like you."

He even offered to pack me some food for when I went ashore.

Captain Smollett asked Silver if he had ever seen the island before on his travels.

"By chance, yes," he said. "Once, I was on another ship when we stopped to fill up our water casks. We were afraid of wild animals attacking, so we slept the night in the safety of a cabin on the island. It's surrounded by a strong wooden stockade."

I knew that the cabin and stockade were marked on the treasure map.

Silver slapped me on the back again and

Looking at Treasure Island.

hopped away. I found it hard to believe the cool cunning of Long John. One moment he talked of friendship, the next of murder.

But now was my chance to tell the others all I had heard. The news stunned them.

"The black-hearted pirate," cried the doctor, "he'll hang for this!"

"Perhaps he'll hang us first," said Captain Smollett. "Silver and his crew outnumber us by a long way."

There were seven of us, all honest men — Captain Smollett, Doctor Livesey, Squire Trelawney, his servants Hunter and Joyce, the gamekeeper Redruth, and me. The pirates numbered at least fifteen or more. I was sure that young lads like Dick would never join Silver.

The captain spoke. "We can't go back. If we try to sail away, they'll kill us all. But we do have time on our side. They won't kill us until they find the map, or discover the treasure."

The captain told us his plan. Silver and his crew would be allowed to go ashore for the afternoon. After a long voyage, there was nothing they would like better. It would also keep them out of the way while we completed the rest of Captain Smollett's plan.

We would then transport guns and supplies

to the island and set up our headquarters in the cabin. The captain thought we could defend ourselves at the cabin far better than we could on the ship.

The crew were delighted to be told they could go ashore. But Silver had decided that he wanted to leave two of his men behind to help guard the ship. Perhaps he was suspicious of what we were up to and wanted to have his spies keep an eye on us.

Israel Hands and O'Brien were the two who stayed behind while Silver and the rest of the crew went ashore in one of the ship's small boats.

We had to play a very clever game now, if we were to survive.

We couldn't leave the ship without dealing with Hands and O'Brien first.

Doctor Livesey solved that problem by giving the two a couple of bottles of rum. They drank it all very quickly and were soon fast asleep. The doctor wasted no time in tying the men up and throwing them in the hold below decks.

Squire Trelawney handed out pistols to everyone. Then we quickly loaded gunpowder, muskets, the medicine chest, and all the food we could carry onto another small boat and set off for the island.

There was one weapon we couldn't take with us. The big ship's cannon was too heavy.

We landed on the beach. There was a terrible smell of rotting tree trunks from the swamp. It was steamy hot without a breath of wind.

Suddenly, from the gloomy marsh, we heard a long, drawn-out scream that echoed around the island. A flock of marsh birds took to the air.

We didn't know what had happened but Captain Smollett ordered everyone to quickly unload the boat.

We hurried inland to find the cabin without being spotted by any of Silver's men.

We saw the stockade first. It was made of rough-hewn tree trunks and was as high as a man's shoulders.

We walked right around the stockade until we found a gate. It wasn't locked.

We walked in and saw the cabin. It stood on a small sandy hill in the middle of the stockade. An overgrown path led to the front door.

The cabin was square with walls made of more tree logs. Narrow windows had been cut into each wall to give those inside a clear

A scream echoed around the island.

musket shot at anyone approaching.

There was no chimney, just a hole in the wooden roof.

Inside, it was very dark and dusty. As my eyes got used to the light, I saw there was just one room. A fireplace stood in the middle.

We quickly unloaded all the things we had brought from the ship. Then we loaded the muskets and leaned them beside the windows ready for action.

Once everything was stored, Doctor Livesey and the others sat down to plan how they would defend the place against the pirates.

As for me, I was free to roam. Everyone was sure that neither Silver nor his men would hurt me. Besides, the pirates were not to know that I knew their secret.

"Jim, you can help us more than anyone," said the doctor. "You can be our spy. Old Silver trusts you."

So I set out to explore the island alone.

The stockade.

Chapter 14
Two Murders

From the cabin, I walked across the clearing into the trees and set off in the general direction of Spy Glass Hill.

I soon found myself in a boggy marsh. I was up to my waist in evil-smelling mud when I saw my first snake. It raised its head and rattled at me like a spinning top. But it let me pass. For sure, it could have overtaken me in the bog if it had chosen to.

Soon after I climbed up onto firmer ground and heard voices coming from behind some trees. I crept closer and found myself beside some bushes on the edge of another small clearing.

I saw Long John Silver first, and lying at his feet was young Dick, a knife buried deep in his back.

It must have been his dying scream we had heard as we landed.

Now Silver was threatening Tom, another young sailor.

"You see what happens if you don't join us."

"Dear Tom," said Silver, in that false way of his. He was pointing to the body. "You see what happens if you don't join us. Now, my boy, I thinks gold dust of you; you're precious to me. So come and join us."

Refusing to join Silver had clearly cost Dick his life. What would Tom do?

"You're no friend of mine, Silver," shouted Tom, as brave as any man. "You've murdered Dick and now you can kill me too, if you can. I'll never join your murderous crew."

With that, he ran for his life.

Silver grabbed his crutch and threw it like a spear. It hit Tom on the head. Tom's arms flew into the air, he gave a sort of gasp and fell to the ground.

He was trying to get to his feet again when Silver wrenched the knife from Dick's body and buried it deep in Tom's.

As he lay dying, Silver pulled out the knife and wiped it clean with a wisp of grass.

"That's two problems dealt with," said Silver.

I was shaking uncontrollably. I wished I had never left the others to explore the island. I was sure I would be Silver's next victim.

I ran off, hoping to find the stockade again.

Leaping between the rocks.

But now I was so terrified I lost my direction. I eventually emerged from the trees and found myself at the foot of Spy Glass Hill.

My heart was still thumping when I heard a noise and saw the strangest sight.

A little way up the hill a figure was leaping with great speed between the rocks. It was as if it was playing hide and seek with me; first appearing from behind a rock and then hiding behind another one.

I could not tell if the figure was a monkey, a man, or whatever.

The weird creature started to circle around me at a distance, as if it wanted to come closer but dare not.

I thought it might be a mountain goat. Then I saw it only had two legs.

It was a man. At last, he stopped moving and, for a moment, we just stared at each other. Then he took a few steps toward me, threw himself onto his knees, and held out his hands.

"Save me! Save me!" he croaked. "I haven't seen or spoken with another man in three years."

"Who are you?" I asked, wide-eyed with astonishment.

"I'm poor Ben Gunn," he said. "A cruelly treated Ben Gunn."

Chapter 15
The Wild Man of the Island

I had never seen such a wreck of a man. His skin had been scorched by the hot sun. His lips were cracked and almost black. His pale eyes were sunken and his hair reached down to his waist. He looked like a wild man.

He was dressed in old rags, held together by bits of stick and loops of rope.

"Were you shipwrecked?" I asked the strange creature.

"No," he answered, "my shipmates left me here. They marooned me. Left me alone for dead and sailed away. Ever since, I've lived on wild goat's milk, berries, and oysters. I would give my life for a piece of cheese ... especially toasted cheese."

I promised he should have all the cheese he wanted if I ever made it back on board our ship again.

These words pleased him greatly. "I've lived rough," he said, "but I'm rich. I'm so rich you'll be pleased you came to my rescue."

I thought the poor fellow was crazy.

"Don't doubt me," he said, seeing my look, "there's no one richer on this island."

Then a shadow passed over his face. He put a finger to his lips and pointed down to the spot when the *Hispaniola* was anchored between Treasure Island and Skeleton Island. "Tell me true, is that Captain Flint's ship?" he asked.

"No," I said, "Captain Flint is long dead. But some of his old crew are here."

"Is there a man with one leg?" he gasped.

"You mean Long John Silver?" I said.

"Aye, Silver was his name."

I said that Silver had come aboard as our cook but that he really was a pirate.

"So he is," said Ben Gunn, nervously, "and if you were sent by Long John, I'm as good as dead meat and I know it!"

The man calmed down when I told him that I was out exploring by myself. I then told him the whole story of our voyage and of my friends Doctor Livesey, the captain, and the squire.

"Would the doctor be generous enough to take me home to England?" he asked. "I can pay him well."

Ben Gunn.

I told him that the doctor was a generous man and, besides, if we defeated the pirates, we would need someone like him to help us sail our ship home.

A grateful smile spread across Ben Gunn's wild and haunted face. Then he started to tell his own story.

Chapter 16
Ben Gunn's Story

Ben Gunn sat on a rock overlooking the distant *Hispaniola* and told me how he had been a member of Captain Flint's crew on board *The Walrus*.

"I was with Billy Bones, Long John Silver, Israel Hands, O'Brien, and Tom Morgan. We were all on that ship."

If I didn't know it already, now I was sure that we had brought Flint's entire gang of cutthroats on our voyage to Treasure Island.

Ben Gunn went on to explain that he had been aboard *The Walrus* on the day that Flint went ashore with six sailors to bury his treasure.

"Flint came back alone with his face white as death," said Ben. "He'd killed all six somehow. There must have been terrible murder done that day. But he didn't want a living soul to know where his treasure was."

Ben Gunn told me how several years later

he was on another ship which passed Treasure Island and the captain had allowed him ashore with some of the crew to search for the treasure.

"We searched for days but found nothing," said Ben. "The captain said I had been wasting his time. So he gave me a musket and a shovel and told me to find the treasure by myself. That's what he said. Then they all left me on this island and sailed away."

Ben said he had survived by trapping animals for food. He had also built himself a small boat to catch fish from.

"Look down there," he said, pointing to a rocky headland which we had passed before dropping anchor. "That's called White Rock. That's where I keep my boat."

Ben Gunn suddenly fell silent for a moment. "And on the beach below that rock," he said solemnly, "that's where I found five skeletons buried. They were the men who helped Flint bury his treasure. I recognized them from the remains of their clothing. But I never found the sixth man."

Ben Gunn's story was interrupted by a sudden explosion out to sea. I looked down toward the *Hispaniola*. Smoke was billowing from the big cannon on the deck.

A flag had been raised on board the ship. It was the Jolly Roger, with its black skull and crossbones . . . the flag of every pirate.

I could see two men at work around the gun although they were too far away to identify. But it must have been Israel Hands and O'Brien. They had obviously escaped from the hold and were firing at Doctor Livesey and the others in the cabin.

Ben Gunn and I watched the drama from Spy Glass Hill. Time and time again there was a puff of smoke and an explosion from the

The flag of every pirate.

cannon on the *Hispaniola's* deck. We watched each cannonball rise into the air and fall to earth near the cabin.

I saw that someone had raised the Union Jack flag on the cabin roof.

"I must get back," I said to Ben Gunn, "but I promise I will tell Doctor Livesey about you."

"You tell him," said Ben Gunn. "Tell him to come and see me at noon on any day. I will be here."

I raced away down the hill toward the clearing where the cabin stood.

As I neared the stockade, I saw Doctor Livesey and the others at the gate. They were about to close it. And I quickly saw the reason why.

Running toward the stockade from the other direction were Silver and his pirates.

"Keep the gate open," I screamed as I ran out into the clearing.

Doctor Livesey saw me at last and shouted at me to run faster.

It was a race between me and the pirates now.

The pirates let off a volley of gunfire at those by the gate. I saw poor Tom Redruth stumble and fall.

Running toward the stockade.

I was just yards away when the squire, our best gun by far, took aim and shot dead a pirate running right beside Silver. Quickly switching to a second gun, he brought down another pirate with his next shot.

That stopped the pirates. They turned about and ran back to the shelter of the woods.

I reached the gate, and safety, at last. We pulled poor Redruth inside and slammed the gate behind us.

Redruth had been the squire's loyal gamekeeper for many years. The squire dropped down on his knees beside him and kissed his hand, crying like a child. Redruth died a few moments later.

The cannon fire from the *Hispaniola* continued all evening, but nothing hit us.

The squire said the cabin could not be seen from the ship, but added that perhaps the pirate Israel Hands was taking aim at the flag on the cabin roof. "Perhaps it would be wiser to take it down," he said.

"I would not lower that flag for any pirate," cried Captain Smollett. "It'll let them know that I care little about their cannon fire."

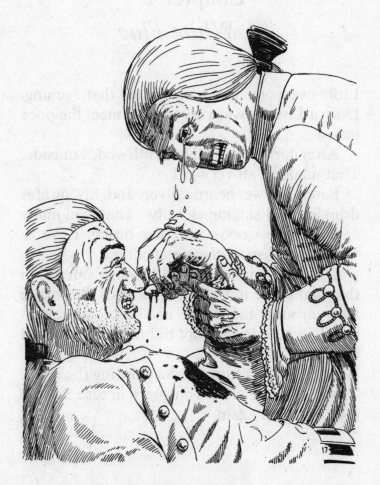

The death of Redruth.

Chapter 17
A White Flag

I told everyone about Ben Gunn that evening. Doctor Livesey was very keen to meet the poor fellow.

After dark we buried Redruth's body outside. That made us all very sad.

Later on we heard Silver and his pirates drinking and singing close by. They had made camp in the woods near the beach, close to where the *Hispaniola* was anchored.

The cold wind whistled through our cabin that night. We lit a fire but most of the smoke blew around the cabin and kept us coughing. The hole in the roof did not make a good chimney.

We took it in turns to sleep during the night. Two of us were always on guard in case Silver's men attacked again.

***

"It's Captain Silver, come to talk."

Early in the morning, I heard someone shouting outside. I jumped up and, rubbing my eyes, looked out of a cabin window.

It was Long John Silver. He was carrying a white flag of truce. I knew this meant he wanted to talk rather than fight.

"It must be a trick," warned Captain Smollett.

"Stand or we fire," shouted the captain. His musket was aimed at Silver's heart.

"It's Captain Silver, come to talk," said the one-legged pirate.

"I don't know anyone called Captain Silver." shouted Captain Smollett. "But I do know a rogue ship's cook called Silver."

"The lads chose me as their captain after you deserted the ship," came the reply. "We weren't to know you would leave us and move into this cabin."

"Deserted the ship, by jove," cried Captain Smollett, "it was our good fortune that we overheard your plans to murder the lot of us."

Silver was quiet for a moment. He had not realized that someone had overheard him plotting.

"Murder you all? Stuff and nonsense!" he bluffed. "Whoever said that is a liar."

Then he threw his crutch over the stockade and climbed over after it. He had trouble walking up the hill to the cabin. His crutch was as helpless as a grounded ship. It kept sinking into the soft sand.

Captain Smollett went forward to meet him.

"Let me go inside by the fire," said Silver. "It's too cold to sit in the sand."

"If you're still my ship's cook, you can warm yourself by the fire," said Captain Smollett, "but if you're Captain Silver, a murdering pirate, then you can go hang."

Silver ignored the remark and looked toward me. "Ah, there's Jim," he said with a false smile. "Top of the morning to you, lad."

"Better say what you want and go," said Captain Smollett.

"Well, here it is," said Silver, sitting down. "We want the treasure. And we'll have it one way or another!"

"The devil you will," answered the captain.

"We don't wish you any harm," continued Silver. "Just give me the map and let us get the treasure. You do that and we'll sail away quietly. We'll even send the first ship we see to pick you up."

Captain Smollett calmly lit his pipe. "Is that

all?" he asked. "You expect me to believe you?"

"Every last word, by thunder," said Silver. "Refuse my offer and the last thing you'll see is a shot from my musket."

"Now hear me," said Captain Smollett. "Fire one shot and I'll clap the lot of you in irons and send you all back to England to hang."

Silver's eyes blazed in anger and he made as if to return to his men. "Give me a hand," he cried, struggling to get up.

"Not I," said the captain.

"Who'll give me a hand up?" roared Silver.

Not a man among us moved.

Growling, Silver crawled over to where his crutch lay. He pulled himself up at last. Then he spat into the ground.

"Within the hour," he cried, "you'll be singing a different tune. Them that die will be the lucky ones. The rest will suffer a fate worse than death."

He stumbled away on his crutch, his parrot screeching on his shoulder.

"Them that die will be the lucky ones."

Chapter 18
The Attack

The captain watched Silver disappear into the woods. Then he gave us his orders. "Right men, do your duty. There's more of them than us, but we can whip them. Take up your muskets."

Doctor Livesey guarded the door. John Hunter took the east window, Joyce the west, and Squire Trelawney watched over the north. The captain guarded the south window.

Spare muskets were loaded and placed by the windows. A large pile of cutlasses was placed by the door ready for hand-to-hand fighting.

My job was to reload the muskets as soon as they were fired.

We waited as the sun climbed into the sky. The day grew hotter and hotter. So the hours passed.

"Where are those cowards?" asked the captain after a while. "I'm getting bored waiting for them."

Swarming over the stockade.

Joyce was the most nervous of us. He thought he saw someone moving in the woods. He took aim and fired.

His shot was still echoing around the clearing when the pirates gave their answer.

A dozen shots rattled out of the woods, peppering the cabin walls. Then all fell deadly quiet. But not for long.

A crowd of screaming pirates leaped from the trees on the north side and ran straight at the stockade.

More gunfire came from the trees to the east and west. One musket shot sang through the cabin doorway and smashed the doctor's musket to bits.

Now the pirates were swarming over the stockade like monkeys. Squire Trelawney, who never missed, toppled three men.

Two fell back into the clearing. One toppled over. More frightened than hurt, he jumped back over the stockade and ran back to the woods.

Four more pirates got over the stockade from the west. They advanced under cover from some furious fire from the woods. They ran up the mound and were outside the cabin before we knew it.

The doctor is attacked.

99

Hunter was pointing his musket out of the window when one of the four grabbed his gun by the barrel. The gun was jerked from Hunter's hands and then smashed in the man's face. Hunter's skull was crushed and he fell to the floor senseless.

A second pirate poked his musket through one of the windows and fired. The shot whistled around the cabin and buried itself in Joyce's head. He died instantly.

A third pirate crashed through the door and attacked the doctor with his cutlass. He gave the doctor a shave with his blade but no serious injury.

The cabin was now full of groans and cries. The cabin was also filling with smoke. We could hardly see to fight.

I heard Silver's voice from outside the cabin. "We've got 'em now boys. Kill 'em all!" he cried.

We were losing the battle. I could see that as I reloaded muskets and pistols as fast as I could.

The captain saw it too.

"Outside, lads and fight them in the open," ordered the captain. "Use your cutlasses!"

Everyone ran for the door and grabbed a

The Attack

Face-to-face with a pirate.

cutlass as they went through. I took one too, but as I picked it up someone else's blade scratched my knuckles. It was my first battle wound.

More pirates were climbing over the stockade now. They carried their cutlasses between their teeth and fired muskets as they advanced.

But they lost their nerve when they saw us come out of the cabin and charge down the hill toward them.

Once outside the cabin door, I came face-to-face with a pirate who slashed at me with his cutlass. I ducked, tripped, and rolled all the way down the slope to the stockade.

My sudden arrival at the stockade only surprised the pirates further. Now we had them on the run. They flung themselves back over the stockade and ran for the woods.

The captain ordered us back to the cabin. From there, the men grabbed their muskets again and put more hot shot into the retreating enemy.

Silver was the last to flee, taking a parting shot at the captain. The musket ball hit the captain's arm.

The battle was over.

At the end of the day there were eight men

dead. We had killed six pirates but two of our men, Joyce and Hunter, were dead.

The captain's injury was not too serious. He would live.

Doctor Livesey examined the scratch on my hand and said it was only a fleabite. He patched it up and pulled my ears in the bargain.

Chapter 19
A Plan

There was no sign of the pirates the next day. So Doctor Livesey took up his pistols, a cutlass, and a musket and set off to find the wild man of the island, Ben Gunn.

With the doctor gone, I fell into a bit of mischief.

Call me a fool, but I was still only a boy and perhaps too adventurous for my own good. But I had a plan.

Without telling anyone, I took a pair of pistols and left the cabin. The first part of my plan was to find White Rock and Ben Gunn's boat.

When I reached the sea, a breeze had sprung up. The surf was tumbling and tossing along the beach. I saw the *Hispaniola* riding up and down on the swell.

It was a long walk to White Rock. By late afternoon, I had found Ben Gunn's boat. It was almost circular in shape and made of a simple

The boat in the water.

wooden frame covered by a goatskin. It looked more like a circular bathtub than a boat. It was a boat they called a coracle.

It was so light that I could carry it on my shoulders. I set off back to the beach with the coracle.

I waited in the trees behind the beach until dusk fell. By then I could see just two things; the blazing fire in the pirate camp farther along the beach and a dim light glimmering on the water offshore. That light came from the *Hispaniola*.

I put the coracle on my back and tiptoed toward the water's edge. Just then I heard the pirates start to sing. How well I knew the words of their song.

"Fifteen men on a dead man's chest,
Yo-ho-ho and a bottle of rum!
Drink and the devil has done for the rest,
Yo-ho-ho and a bottle of rum!"

I slipped the boat into the water and climbed aboard. I took the paddle and set off toward the *Hispaniola*.

I soon discovered that Ben Gunn's coracle had a mind of its own. It twisted and turned in every direction but the one I wanted it to go in.

I would never have reached the ship by

A furious argument.

paddling alone. Luckily, the tide pushed me close.

At last the ship loomed out of the darkness. The light I had seen was coming from the window of the captain's cabin at the back. It cast a ghostly light on the water.

I heard loud voices coming from the cabin.

I tied my boat to the anchor rope and, pulling myself up hand over hand, reached the cabin window.

I looked in and saw Israel Hands and O'Brien. The two pirates were having a furious argument. Each had a grip upon the other's throat. I had no idea what they were fighting about. But then the pirates, when they weren't fighting us, always seemed to be arguing with one another.

But I couldn't care. I scrambled down the anchor rope and climbed into my little craft again. Now it was time to complete my plan.

I took out my cutlass and sliced the ship's anchor rope, setting the *Hispaniola* adrift.

Chapter 20
At Sea in a Small Boat

The *Hispaniola* gave a violent groan and spun around the instant I cut the anchor rope.

That caught me by surprise. I now had my feet in the coracle, which was bobbing up and down, and my hands holding onto the rolling ship.

I didn't know whether to risk falling back into the coracle or try to jump back onto the ship.

The ship and the coracle now moved swiftly down the narrow strip of water between Skeleton Island and Treasure Island. The seas became rougher as the rising tide pushed everything in its path toward the wide ocean beyond.

The little coracle started to spin and turn again, violently racing up and down the ever bigger waves. It was now or never. If I didn't let go of the ship I would soon be miles out to sea.

Suddenly, I heard the voices of O'Brien and Hands coming from the cabin above me. The two pirates had at last realized the ship was adrift and heading out to sea. They were in a terrible panic.

I certainly had no plans to go with them. So I finally let go of the ship and slipped down into the coracle.

The *Hispaniola* quickly slipped away into the foggy blackness.

Now I was alone and very frightened. I prayed for the wind and the tide to push me ashore. There was no way I could row myself against that tide.

Ben Gunn's coracle wasn't listening to my prayers. It tossed and turned on the waves and went spinning farther out to sea.

I saw the dim light of the mutineers' campfire slowly fade on the distant shore. I headed toward deeper and ever rougher seas.

There was nothing I could do now but await my fate. So I lay all night in the bottom of the violently rocking boat, hoping that I wouldn't drown and be in Davy Jones's Locker by morning.

I was so exhausted from worry that I eventually fell deeply asleep. I dreamed of my mother and the Admiral Benbow Inn.

The coracle spun farther out to sea.

***

The chilly, misty dawn found me soaked and freezing cold. I had drifted a long way out to sea, although I could just see Treasure Island in the far distance.

The sun rose and warmed my frozen bones a little. More importantly, the tide began to turn.

I started to paddle again. Still the boat refused to go in the direction I wanted. So I gave up once more.

That's when I discovered that the little circular boat was best left to find its own way home.

It surprised me to see how easily the boat rode the waves. Each wave became like the hills and valleys on shore. Magically, the boat threaded its way through the valleys and avoided the steep slopes.

The boat slowly made her own way back toward the shore.

The sun was getting warmer and the last of the morning mist had burned away.

Then suddenly, I saw the *Hispaniola* again. She was charging through the waves toward me with all sails flying.

Her white sails shone in the sun like silver.

Jim jumped onto the ship.

The skull and crossbones still fluttered on her main mast.

At first I thought that Hands and O'Brien were now chasing after me. Then I saw the ship was sailing a very strange course. She was zigzagging from side to side as if no one was steering her.

"Clumsy fellows," I thought, "they'll be wrestling again."

The more I watched, the more I wondered if the men had abandoned ship. Maybe there was no one left on board to steer.

It was time to act before I was run down and drowned. I decided I had to board her.

The *Hispaniola* swept closer and closer toward me. Round she came. For a brief moment she was alongside me, rising and falling with the sea swell.

I had no time to think now. I waited until the ship had raced down one wave and then jumped, just as she started to rise on the next.

I caught hold of the railings on the side and hauled myself up onto the deck.

I looked down to see Ben Gunn's coracle struck several times by the *Hispaniola*.

The gallant little boat which had taken me to sea and back broke up into little pieces.

My fate now lay aboard the pirate ship.

Chapter 21
Down with the Jolly Roger

There was no sign of Israel Hands or O'Brien. It was a ghost ship.

Broken rum bottles lay everywhere. The decks hadn't been scrubbed since we left. The cabins had been torn apart and wrecked during the search for the treasure map.

The huge sails flapped in the rigging above me. There was not a soul to be seen.

Suddenly the wind changed. The ship creaked and shuddered. The steering wheel spun as if an invisible sailor was turning it.

The sails, which had hidden my view of part of the rear deck, filled with wind. They rose like a curtain to reveal Hands and O'Brien.

O'Brien was lying with his arms stretched out on either side of him. His mouth was wide open and his grinning teeth gleamed in the sunlight. He was dead, for sure. Hands must have killed him in a fight.

Hands himself was in a sitting position

beside O'Brien. His chin was on his chest, and his arms lay motionless. He had a nasty wound to his leg.

His normally dark-skinned face was now ghostly white. The deck around him was stained with blood. He had fired his last cannon ball, I thought.

I was wondering what to do next when I heard a low moan. Hands wasn't dead. He raised a hand as if asking for help.

I could feel no sympathy for old Israel Hands. I remembered the night I hid in the apple barrel and overheard him and Silver planning to murder us all.

He looked at me and grunted. "Aye. And where might you have come from?"

"Well," I said, "I've come aboard to take possession of this ship. I'm your captain now."

He looked at me sourly, but said nothing as I went to the mast and hauled down the Jolly Roger and threw it overboard. "God save the King!" I cried. "And there's an end to Captain Silver."

Old Hands watched me with a sly eye, as I raised the Union Jack. "Cap'n Hawkins," he said, "I'm done for. I'm your prisoner now. If you want to get back to your friends, I can help you."

Hands and O'Brien.

"Speak up then," I replied, trying to make myself sound as bold as Captain Smollett.

"If you give me food and drink and an old scarf to tie up my wounds," said Hands, "I'll show you how to sail this ship back to the island."

Throwing the Jolly Roger overboard.

Hands picked out a well-bloodied knife.

119

I wanted the ship back on the island, but not where Silver and his men could find it.

"I accept your offer of help," I said, "but we'll need to beach her because we haven't got an anchor now."

"We can do that in North Cove," he said.

I knew from the treasure map that the cove was on the other side of the island. Silver was unlikely to find the ship there.

Hands stuck to his bargain and told me how to turn the ship around. Soon we were sailing along the east coast of Treasure Island.

Hands didn't move from where he lay, but kept his beady eye on me all the time. He kept smiling and running his tongue over his lips. I didn't trust him at all despite his promise to help.

Then he asked me to go below deck and find him a drink. "I'm a-dying of thirst," he said.

He was up to no good. But I played along with his game. "A rum?" I asked.

"A glass of something strong and plenty of it, Jim, my old shipmate," he said.

I hurried below deck. But then I took off my shoes and sneaked back to see what he was up to.

For a half-dead sailor, he moved pretty

Charging at Jim with a terrifying roar.

quickly. Hands got to his feet and, trailing his wounded leg behind him, scurried across the deck. I saw him open a box and pick out a well-bloodied knife. He slipped it into his shirt. Then he moved back to where I had left him.

I returned with his drink. I knew I was safe for the moment. It needed both of us to sail the ship for now. But as we moved closer to the shore, I watched his every move.

Hands was a vile pirate and murderer, but he was also a good sailor. As we sailed into North Cove, he spied the best place to beach the ship and even explained how the ship could be re-floated at high tide.

The closer we came to the beach, the closer I watched Hands. I knew he had to make his move soon.

I was steadying myself for the boat running onto the beach when I saw him slowly get to his feet again.

Out came his knife. He charged at me with a terrifying roar.

Chapter 22
Pieces of Eight

I was ready for Hands and his knife. I turned and pulled the pistols from my belt.

"Stop where you are!" I cried, pointing the guns at his head.

Like a maddened bull, he kept on. I had no choice. I pulled the triggers.

Nothing happened. The gunpowder was damp.

The wily old sea dog now had me trapped against the mast. Twice he jabbed the knife at me, twice I jumped aside.

The third time he stabbed, I jumped and he drove the knife into the mast.

I ran off down the deck as he tried to pull out the knife. I had to find time to reload my pistols.

Then the ship hit the beach with a huge crunch. We were both tossed to the deck as the ship heeled over. It came to rest at a steep angle. I recovered first and climbed up the main mast.

Hands came after me. His injuries slowed him down and I was well ahead by the time I reached the crow's nest. I leapt in and started to reload my pistols. Closer and closer he came, his fearsome knife clenched between his teeth.

At last my pistols were reloaded. "One more step, Hands," I warned, pointing both pistols at him again, "and I'll blow your brains out. Dead men don't bite, if you remember."

The look on Hands's face showed he remembered the time by the apple barrel, when he agreed with Silver that it was better to kill us all rather than maroon us on a desert island.

He took the knife from his mouth. "Jim, my boy," he said, "I'm done for. You've got me. I'll surrender for sure this time. But I tell you, it's hard for a master sailor like me to admit he's been beaten by a mere cabin boy."

I smiled. I was so proud of myself. I had single-handedly captured one of the pirates.

Oh, how wrong I was.

In one lightning movement, his hand went back over his shoulder. Something sang through the air like an arrow. I felt a blow and then a sharp pain.

And there I was, pinned to the mast by Hands's long-bladed dagger.

Jim dodged the knife.

I reacted by instinct. My fingers pulled the triggers and both my pistols went off.

Hands let out a choked cry. A shot hit him above the ear. He let go of the rope he was holding and fell headfirst. His body clattered through the rigging

Such was the angle of the ship that he didn't hit the deck. He plunged straight into the sea. I saw him sink and then rise to the surface in a lather of foam and blood. Then he disappeared for good.

***

The knife had pinned me to the mast by a pinch of skin. With a violent shudder, I ripped myself free. The blood ran freely.

I climbed down to the deck and tied the wound with an old piece of cloth.

O'Brien's body was still lying on the deck. I picked him up by his waist belt and dragged his body across the deck. Then I dropped it over the side, into the water.

O'Brien drifted down to join Israel Hands in Davy Jones's Locker.

I dived into the sea and swam ashore.

I was shaken by all that had just happened but my spirits were high.

Both pistols went off.

127

The ship was ours. It was ready for us to board and go to sea again. Captain Smollett would be proud of me. At first they might blame me for leaving without a word. But once I told them about the *Hispaniola,* they would be pleased.

It was night by the time I approached the cabin again. The breeze whistled quietly through the trees and the moon came out just as I reached the stockade clearing.

I started to worry when I saw that there was no guard outside the cabin. That was unusual because Captain Smollett always liked to have the cabin guarded at night. I suspected something was wrong.

I crept closer. I heard a noise. Then I started to smile. It was like music to my ears. It was the sound of snoring coming from inside.

I sneaked into the cabin determined not to wake anyone. I wanted to see their surprise in the morning.

I tripped on someone's foot. All of a sudden, a shrill voice cried out. "Pieces of eight! Pieces of eight!"

It was Silver's parrot, Cap'n Flint.

Then I heard a mighty roar. "Who goes there?"

Drifting down to Davy Jones's Locker.

A hand came out of the darkness and caught me tightly by the neck.

The hand belonged to Long John Silver.

"Who goes there?"

Chapter 23
In the Enemy's Camp

The red glare of a lantern suddenly lit up the cabin. The pirates had taken over the cabin again. There sat Silver, Morgan, and four other pirates.

There was no sign of any prisoners. I could only think that all my friends had been killed.

The parrot sat preening its feathers on Silver's shoulder. "Shiver me timbers, Jim Hawkins has dropped by," said Silver. "That's very friendly of you, Jim."

Silver looked at me very closely. "I knew you were clever when I first set eyes on you. But maybe you're cleverer than I thought."

I wondered how much he knew. Did he know that I had overheard him talking by the apple barrel? Did he know I had killed Hands? Did he know I had recaptured the ship?

Silver continued talking. "Seeing that you're here, I'll give you a piece of my mind. I've always liked you, Jim. You've got spirit. You remind me of when I was young."

This murdering pirate always had a way of making you think that perhaps he wasn't as evil as you thought he was.

"I always wanted you to join us and take your share of the treasure," he continued. "That way you could be a gentleman of fortune. That's a good name for a pirate, eh?"

Silver put his arm around me. "Even Doctor Livesey has gone against you," he said. "You went off and left him. He thinks you've joined us. So you can't go back to him now. You'll have to join Captain Silver. You can live or die as a gentleman of fortune. Which is it to be, my lad?"

That sounded like a death sentence to me. But I was glad to hear that my friends were still alive somewhere.

Silver hadn't finished. "The doctor came down to our camp yesterday and told us that the *Hispaniola* had gone. So we had a look for the ship and by thunder, it was gone. Then the doctor said he wanted to make a bargain."

"And what was that?" I asked.

"We could have this cabin, the food and, if we ever see it again, the ship," answered Silver.

"What did you give Doctor Livesey in return?" I asked.

"You'll have to join Captain Silver."

133

"His life," Silver replied. "Nothing else. Now the ship's gone, the doctor said there was no point in fighting."

"What about me?" I asked.

Silver told me that I was not included in the deal. "The doctor said you'd deserted your duty. He said he didn't care what happened to you. He said he was sick of you. Them was his words."

That hurt me to the heart. I knew all along I should never have left the doctor and the others. But all my plans had worked out. I was sure they would forgive me when they heard what I had done.

Now I felt very alone; a prisoner of the pirates and my friends not wanting to see me again.

"If only the doctor knew the truth," I shouted at Silver, "he wouldn't be angry at me."

"What's the truth?" he asked.

"You've lost your ship," I blurted out. "Do you know who was responsible for that?"

A strange look came over his face. The truth was dawning on him.

"Yes, it was me!" I cried.

I couldn't stop myself now. I told him the whole story; how I was in the apple barrel the

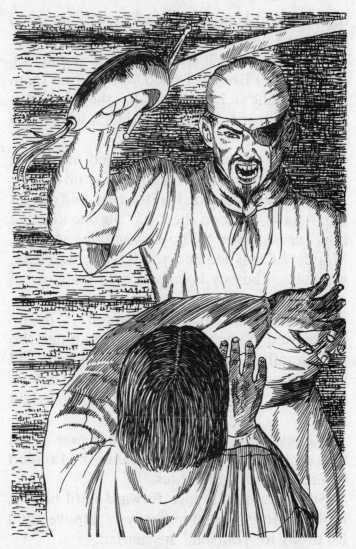

"Kill the boy now!"

night he and Hands spoke of murdering us all and how I had told the doctor.

"And if you're looking for your shipmates, Israel and O'Brien," I cried, "you'll find them in Davy Jones's Locker. As for the ship, I cut her anchor rope. Now she's hidden where you won't find her."

A pirate called Morgan stepped out at me with his cutlass raised. "Kill the boy now!"

Silver flung his crutch at the man and caught him a nasty blow on the ear. "No one kills the boy!" cried Silver. "Who do you think you are, Morgan? Cross me and you'll walk the plank, shipmate. The boy is more a man than any of you rats."

But Morgan stood his ground. "Silver," he snarled, "you've lost us everything. We want another captain; otherwise we'll all end up dancing on the end of a rope in Execution Dock. Perhaps we should hang you right now."

I knew where Execution Dock was. That was a place on the River Thames in London where they hanged pirates.

Silver stepped a pace forward until he was looking Morgan right in the eye. "You've got a lot to say for yourself," he snarled.

"I know my rights," answered Morgan. "We can choose a new captain. And we will. We're about sick of you and that boy."

With that, Morgan led the others out of the cabin. "We'll have our vote on it now," he shouted.

"Never mind them dogs," said Silver when they'd gone. "They'll never hang me. I've still got a card up my sleeve."

Chapter 24
A Secret, a Promise and a Warning

"Step up lads, I won't eat you," cried Silver, when the men returned after voting on who should be captain.

Silver took the pirates aside and talked quietly to them, thinking I could not hear what he was saying. But I could.

"Look," he whispered, "I agree with you all. I'd sooner kill the boy for what he has done. But he's our hostage. We can use him. No one will hang us while we have the boy."

Morgan stepped forward. "It's too late for you Silver," he said. "We've made our minds up. You'll have to go."

"And you're to be captain, are you?" said Silver.

"Aye," replied Morgan.

"And what are you going to do about me then," said Silver, boldly. "Hang me?"

"We haven't made our minds up yet," said Morgan.

The pirates had the treasure map.

Silver put his hand in his shirt pocket and produced a piece of paper. He quietly laid it on the floor between Morgan and himself.

"Now," said Silver, "I think that bit of paper might make your friends change their minds about who should be captain."

I recognized the piece of paper instantly.

"Now tell me I've lost everything," said Silver. "Have a look at that, you old sea dogs! It's something that Doctor Livesey gave me. It looks like a treasure map to me."

It was the treasure map! I could see the red cross in the middle. It was the same map that I had found at the Admiral Benbow Inn at the bottom of Billy Bones's sea chest.

The pirates jumped on it like a cat on a mouse. It went from hand to hand. They started laughing and cheering. You might have thought they had already found the gold and were back at sea on their way home.

As for me, I could not believe that Doctor Livesey had given up the treasure map without a reason.

Silver was triumphant. "You sea dogs lost the ship, but I found the treasure map. Who's the best man for captain now?"

"Captain Silver," they all cried.

Without a word, he went to his patient.

"You said you wanted a new captain," he teased. "You cutthroats. You'd sell your own mothers for that map."

There was no disputing who was still captain. Morgan got a good beating from the captain that night for calling on the others to mutiny.

"Another word against me," Silver warned Morgan afterwards, "and you'll walk the plank. I'll feed you to the fishes."

***

In the morning, there was a surprise visitor to the cabin. It was Doctor Livesey. He had come to treat one of the pirates who had been wounded in the attack on the cabin a few days earlier.

"Where's the patient?" said the doctor. "Good man or bad, I have a duty as a doctor to help everyone."

He looked at Silver with a threatening eye. "I'll even keep a man alive long enough to face the hangman on the gallows."

"And top of the morning to you, doctor," Silver replied, pretending to ignore the remark. "We have a surprise for you today. A new lodger."

"Who's that?" he asked.

"Jim," laughed Silver.

"Jim Hawkins?"

"Himself," said Silver, calling me forward.

The doctor frowned when he saw me. I could see that I had disappointed him by running off. If only I had the chance to tell him what I had done. But without a word, he went over to his patient.

Afterwards, Silver took the doctor to one side and told him how he had saved my life when Morgan tried to cut me down with his cutlass. "I hope you'll remember that, doctor," said Silver, "if I ever come to trial in Execution Dock."

"Why should I?" asked the doctor.

"I'm no coward," answered Silver, "but I can see the gallows. I can feel the rope twisting around my neck. I just want you to speak up for me and tell 'em how I saved his life once . . . it might save my life."

The doctor promised he would do what he could. Silver then said I could have a few words with the doctor in private if I promised not to escape.

***

"Why did you do it, Jim?" the doctor asked me when we were alone. "Why did you run away and desert us?"

I was in tears. "Spare me, Doctor. I am a hostage. And they might torture me."

A tear came to the doctor's eye. "I can't find it in my heart to blame you," he said. "Come on. We'll make a run for it."

Sadly, I told the doctor I could not break my word to Silver and try to escape.

"That two-timing rogue Silver doesn't know the meaning of a promise," said the doctor, angrily.

But he saw I would not change my mind and, instead, asked me if they had threatened me with torture.

"For sure, they will torture me to find out where I left the ship," I said.

"The ship!" he cried, excitedly. "You know where the ship is?"

"I am the only one alive who does," I said.

I told the doctor all that had happened since leaving the cabin.

"And we thought you had deserted us," he said. "All that time you were risking your life. Every step, it's you that saves our lives. You discovered Silver's plot. You found Ben Gunn, which may turn out to be the best thing you ever did in your life. And now you have stolen the ship from under their noses."

Silver joined us again. He looked back to the cabin to make sure none of the pirates could hear him. Then he asked the doctor a question. It was a question that I wanted answering, too.

"We'll make a run for it."

145

"Tell me plain," he said, "why did you and your men leave the cabin without so much as a fight? And why did you give me the treasure map?"

"Silver, I would tell you why," said the doctor, "but those secrets belong to someone else. Instead, I'll give you two warnings."

The doctor looked Silver straight in the eye. "First, when you go looking for the treasure, be very, very careful. Things might not be what they seem. And secondly, keep Jim close by you at all times. One thing's for sure, Silver, if Jim dies, you'll hang."

Chapter 25
The Treasure Hunt

"So Jim," Silver said to me, as we returned to the cabin, "you and me must stick close, back to back like. I'll save your neck, and you may save mine from a hanging."

There never was a man like Silver for always changing sides, or even trying to stay friends with both sides at once. He had made a deal with the doctor to save his own skin. Now it was time to please his men.

"Right, me old shipmates," he said, holding up the treasure map, "it's time to go a-treasure hunting."

The pirates cheered. They were sure they would all be rich by noon.

For myself, I still wondered why my friends had left the cabin and why the doctor didn't seem worried that Silver had the map.

Silver kept close to me. He tied a rope tightly around my waist and tied the other end to his belt.

"That'll keep him as safe as gold," he told the other pirates. "We can use him as a hostage if we have trouble with Captain Smollett and his men."

We set off after breakfast. The pirates carried picks, shovels, and food. Silver was fully armed with two muskets, a pistol on both hips, and a huge cutlass at his waist. Cap'n Flint, the parrot, sat squawking on his shoulder as usual.

I remembered the instructions on the back of the treasure map as if they had been carved on my heart.

Start Skeleton Island. Big tree. North-west to Spy Glass Hill. Tall tree. Ten paces south.

So I wasn't surprised when we all boarded two small boats and rowed across to Skeleton Island.

"Look for a big tree," Silver called out.

The men spread out in a fan shape to search the island. A few minutes later we heard a cry of terror. It sounded like Morgan's voice.

We ran over to find Morgan standing by a huge tree. His face was deathly white. A skeleton lay at his feet.

Those bones sent a chill through every heart. A few strands of pale hair remained on the skull. The leg bones were very long and some

A skeleton at his feet.

shreds of blue sailors' clothing still clung to the skeleton.

This man had been a sailor for sure.

"Bless me, it's Mr. Allardyce," said Silver, as calmly as if he was saying good morning. "Tall man. Light hair. He was one of the six men who went with Cap'n Flint to bury the treasure. You remember him, Morgan, don't you?"

"Aye, I remember him," said Morgan, hunting through what looked like the remains of a trouser pocket, "he owed me money."

But Morgan found nothing among the bones. "This is very strange," he said, "there ain't a thing left. Not a coin. No cutlass. That's not natural. There's something mighty strange about this 'ere skeleton."

We all knew it too. Every one of us saw how the skeleton was lying in a strange way.

The bones of one arm lay beside the rest of the skeleton. The bones of the other lay as if they were pointing to something in the other direction.

It was almost as if someone had arranged the bones in a special position.

Silver took out his compass and placed it alongside the bones of the pointing arm. The pointer beneath the glass turned, wavered and then came to rest. It was pointing north-west.

"Praise the stars!" said Silver. "This is one of Flint's jokes. He always was a black-hearted joker. If I'm not mistaken, these arm bones are pointing straight to the treasure."

Captain Flint had left a skeleton to show us the way.

Chapter 26
The Voice Among the Trees

If Ben Gunn had found the skeletons of five of the six men who helped Flint bury his treasure, then this was the sixth man.

The skeleton's fingers pointed north-west across the water toward Spy Glass Hill. Long John Silver checked the reading on his compass again.

"Looking from here," he said, "a straight line to Spy Glass Hill passes right through the red cross on the map. We're halfway to our treasure already!"

Silver then gave a slight bow. "Thank you, Mr. Allardyce, you've been a great help to us. Good day to you."

We left poor Mr. Allardyce's bones and rowed back to Treasure Island. Silver took new compass readings. These put us directly on the line the skeleton had shown us. Now we set off to look for the second clue on the map . . . a big tree near Spy Glass Hill.

Keeping close to each other.

The skeleton had truly frightened the pirates. They kept close to each other and spoke in quiet whispers as if Allardyce's ghost was following behind.

Silver saw they were afraid. "Flint took six men to help bury his treasure," he reminded the men. "He killed them all too. All that's left of them is bones. They can't hurt you now."

The men still looked nervously around.

"Come on lads, there's nothing to worry about," he continued. "Allardyce and the other five are all dead. They're well gone. And dead men don't walk ... well, not during the day, anyway."

That only scared them more.

We walked on. Even I couldn't get the thought of Allardyce's skeleton out of my mind.

We were now closing in on the area marked out by the red cross. Silver checked his compass again. We were still on the exact line. Ahead lay Spy Glass Hill and, just this side of it, was a clump of tall trees.

We looked for the tallest.

"Shiver me timbers," said Silver, "we're almost there. We'll have the treasure before lunch."

"It's Flint's voice!"

"I don't know," whispered Morgan. "The thought of what Captain Flint did here is giving me the shivers."

It was as if Flint heard his words and answered from the grave. A voice echoed out from the trees in front.

"Fifteen men on a dead man's chest,
Yo-ho-ho and a bottle of rum."

The blood drained from the men's faces. "It's Flint's voice!" cried Morgan. "He always sang that song!"

The song stopped as suddenly as it had begun.

"Don't worry, lads," said Silver, struggling to get his words out, "it's someone skylarking about. Whoever's singing that song is flesh and blood, not dead."

The voice broke out again. It turned to a ghostly, wailing echo. "Bring me a rum, Billy Bones," it cried, "just one last rum for an old sea dog."

"That fixes it," said Morgan. "I'm off. Those were Flint's last words. We all remember those words as he lay dying on his ship."

Even Silver was frightened now, although he tried not to show it. I heard his teeth rattling in his head.

"Stay where you are, shipmates," he ordered. "I'll not be stopped by man nor devil. I was never scared of Flint when he was alive. And I won't be scared of him now he's dead and gone to Davy Jones's Locker. There's the biggest pile of gold buried somewhere here and we're going to find it."

Greedy thoughts of gold seemed to calm the men down.

"Come to think of it," Silver added, "that voice is like Flint's, I grant you, but it's not the same."

He grunted and hobbled off on his crutch. Then he stopped again. "Bless my bones," he said suddenly, "that was Ben Gunn's voice!"

"So it was," cried Morgan. "But Ben was marooned many a year ago. He'll be more dead than Flint."

"Dead or alive, no one minds Ben Gunn," said Silver, who was determined to get his men to hurry on. "Old Ben was as gentle as a lamb. Come on men, forget the voices. That tree there, halfway up the hill—that's the tallest around here. Come on, lads."

Silver tucked his crutch under his arm and hopped away as fast as ever with his parrot on his shoulder and me tied behind.

When we got to the tree Silver examined his compass again. In the distance, we could just see the tree where Allardyce's skeleton lay. The line was exact.

"Now for the last and least puzzling of the clues," said Silver, "ten paces south."

Silver followed his compass pointer and paced it out. He had gone six steps when he reached some thick bushes. "Now, shipmates," he called, waving his crutch in the air. "Take a walk behind the bushes and have your spades ready to dig."

We hurried around the bushes.

What I saw before me shook me as much as it did the others. The pirates could not believe what they had found.

Chapter 27
The Trap

We stood looking into a great empty hole. The sides had fallen in and grass had sprouted at the bottom. All that was left was a shovel broken in two, and a length of wood with the name of Flint's ship, *Walrus*, branded on it. Someone had been here before us. The treasure was gone.

The pirates leapt into the pit, screaming terrible oaths. Some clawed at the earth with their fingers. Morgan found a single gold coin and held it up in the air.

The others stared at it glumly. It was the only one they would find that day.

Silver and I watched from above. His face showed that he too was shocked at finding the treasure gone. But he kept his head.

"Quick, Jim," he whispered, "stand by for trouble."

"So you've changed sides again," I said.

"Rightly so," laughed Silver. "It could save my life."

Silver stood beside me on one side of the hole as the five pirates clambered out on the other side. Now we stood looking at each other.

"Silver?" screamed Morgan, suddenly. "You knew there was no treasure left. You'll die for this!"

"Don't push me, lads," snarled Silver, "I never knew that."

"You're a cheating no-good sea dog," spat Morgan, "now it's us five against you two. I'm done with you, Silver, and I'm also going to cut the boy's heart out of him."

The pirates grabbed their pistols and took aim.

"Sorry, Jim," said Silver, putting his arm around me. "The game's up."

We both waited to die.

Three shots rang out.

They didn't come from Morgan and the pirates' guns, nor from ours. The shots came from the bushes behind us.

Morgan died instantly and tumbled forward into the treasure pit. Another pirate was hit. He spun around dead and fell on top of Morgan.

The last three pirates raced away through the trees and disappeared.

At the same time four men emerged from

160

The Trap

Morgan found a single gold coin.

behind the bushes. Three were carrying smoking muskets. It was Doctor Livesey, Captain Smollett, and Squire Trelawney.

Behind them followed a fourth man. It was Ben Gunn.

Silver was astonished. "So you're still alive, you old dog," he roared. "It was your voice that spooked the men. I only hope you remember that it wasn't me to blame for you being marooned on this island."

The one-legged pirate never lost a chance to prove his innocence. If I didn't know him so well, I'd have thought he was as innocent as a babe in arms.

"Getting me marooned is one of the few crimes you didn't commit," said Ben Gunn, who then revealed to us the mystery of what had happened to the treasure.

"Many years I spent alone, roaming this place," he began. "I came to know every step of it. I knew that treasure had to be somewhere. I eventually stumbled on this place. Years had passed since Flint had buried it, but I could still see where the earth had been dug."

So Ben Gunn had found the treasure long ago and taken it for himself.

Some other things became clearer that morning.

Morgan died instantly.

163

I remembered the day that I had left the cabin. That was the same time that Doctor Livesey had gone off to see Ben Gunn. The doctor explained what had happened when he met Ben Gunn.

"Ben told me he had dug up the treasure already. He told me that he had dug up the treasure and hidden it somewhere else. That made the map useless so I gave it to you, Silver. After all, you did say you wanted it. Then we set up this ambush and waited for you to come to us."

"You're a clever man," said Silver. "I'm glad I listened to your advice and kept young Jim Hawkins close by me. Otherwise one of those three shots of yours might have been aimed at me. And you would never have given it a thought."

Doctor Livesey smiled. "Not a thought," he replied cheerily.

The squire interrupted to give Silver some good news. He would not be sent back to London to face trial in Execution Dock.

"You're a pirate, a villain, and a murderer," he said. "You have roamed the high seas with nothing but greed in your heart. Yet you have saved Jim's life. For that we are grateful. So your neck is safe for now."

"Jim's a good lad," said Silver. "I'm glad to have been of service."

The squire wasn't finished. "Silver, you are the most cunning man I ever met. You'd sell your mother's soul to escape the hangman. You'd better behave now. It's your last chance."

"I'm your man," answered Silver, with a twinkle in his eye. "I resign my title as Captain. I'll do my duty as a ship's cook. To be sure, I'll spend the rest of my life cooking bacon and porridge."

None of us believed a word of what he said.

That night we took the two small boats and sailed around the island to the North Cove where I had beached the *Hispaniola.*

The tide was in. And what's more the ship had floated off the beach by herself.

We waded out and clambered aboard. We had one more important voyage to make . . . to Ben Gunn's treasure cave.

Chapter 28
The Treasure at Last

That evening we anchored the ship opposite Rum Cave near White Rock. This had been Ben Gunn's home for many years.

A gentle slope ran up from the beach to the entrance. My eyes took a little time to get used to the darkness inside. It was large and airy with a small pool of clear mountain water. The floor was sandy and a small fire was burning in the middle.

In one corner, glinting in the light of the fire, were great heaps of coins. And behind them were even bigger piles of gold bars reaching to the ceiling of the cave. This was Flint's treasure. This was what we had come so far to find.

What would old Captain Billy Bones have made of such a treasure trove? He would certainly have reached for a glass of rum!

Silver stared and stared. His face grew dark. It would have been all his if things had turned out differently.

The treasure in Rum Cave.

Captain Flint had killed the six pirates who had helped him bury the treasure. Silver would have likely killed his crew—and me too, once they had dug it up again.

That night we ate supper in the cave. Ben Gunn cooked us salted wild goat over the fire. It was delicious. But Ben's delight that night was a small hoard of cheese we had found on board the *Hispaniola.*

"I have dreamed of cheese for so long," he said, biting into the first piece of cheese he had tasted since he was marooned. "It's worth more to me that all the gold in this cave."

Ben Gunn spent the whole of the next day helping us to carry the gold to the shoreline. It was then ferried to the *Hispaniola.*

I stayed in the cave with Silver for the next few days putting all the coins into great sacks.

At last every gold and silver bar, guinea, dollar, and doubloon was loaded aboard. And in case Silver was feeling greedy, we locked it away in the hold.

The final thing we had to worry about was the fate of the three pirates who had escaped the ambush. The men were now running wild on the island.

The good Doctor Livesey wanted to help

them. But Silver warned him against that. "They'll kill you, for sure," he said.

I wondered whether Silver was only worried for his own skin. The last people he would want to meet were those three.

The search for the treasure had already cost the lives of so many who had set out from Bristol on the *Hispaniola.*

And I wondered how many more had been hanged, made to walk the plank, or been run through with a cutlass over the years, while Flint was collecting that vast treasure.

We decided it wasn't worth risking anyone else's life after all that had happened. The three pirates would have to stay on the island. Besides, if we had taken them home, they would only have been hanged in Execution Dock. We left them a good store of gunpowder, shot, medicines, tools, clothing, and rope. That was our last deed on the island.

In the evening, we boarded the ship and raised the sails. The sun was sinking fast as we weighed anchor and set sail for home.

We were passing the last headland on Treasure Island when we spotted the three pirates. They saw us and dropped to their knees on the sand. Their arms were raised. They cried out and begged us not to leave them to die on the island.

Our ship kept sailing on. Now, they aimed their muskets and sent a cloud of shot whistling over Silver's head.

We rushed for cover; all except Long John Silver. When I looked up, I saw him waving farewell with a sly smile on his lips and his parrot, as ever, on his shoulder.

The sun sank and the last I saw of Treasure Island was Spy Glass Hill standing out against a blood-colored, scarlet sunset.

Treasure Island finally disappeared below the horizon.

They begged us not to leave them.

Chapter 29

Home Again

Long John Silver's story was not finished yet.

On the way home, we dropped anchor at a port in South America to take on fresh water. While we were there, we had supper aboard an English warship.

Ben Gunn and Silver stayed on the *Hispaniola* to guard the ship. We returned to find that Silver and his parrot had gone. Ben Gunn confessed to having helped Silver escape.

"It was for the best," said Ben. "If he had stayed aboard, he would likely have killed one or more of us before we got home."

Silver hadn't gone empty-handed. He had broken into the hold and removed a large sack of gold. Once a pirate always a pirate, so they say.

We were all glad to see him go, really.

I never heard another word of Long John Silver. Yet, a tiny part of me often wondered about that one-legged gentleman of fortune. No doubt, he joined another pirate ship.

"Pieces of eight! Pieces of eight!"

173

When we got home to England most of Flint's gold was taken for the King's treasure chest. But we were given a good reward.

Ben Gunn was given a pouch of gold for his troubles too. He now lives a quiet life, goes to church every Sunday, and has cheese for supper most nights.

For myself, I will be happy for any man to call me a landlubber now. I never want to go back to sea again. I have seen enough of it.

Whenever I hear the surf booming on the shore beneath the Admiral Benbow Inn, I can still hear the sharp voice of Silver's parrot, screeching out: "Pieces of eight! Pieces of eight!"

And as for Black Dog, Blind Pew, Billy Bones, and Long John Silver, they will sail through my nightmares for the rest of my life.